W9-AWV-859

Reycraft Books
55 Fifth Avenue
New York, NY 10003

Reycraftbooks.com

Reycraft Books is a trade imprint and trademark of
Newmark Learning, LLC.

This edition is published by arrangement with Hsiao
Lu Publishing Co., Ltd. © Hsiao Lu Publishing Co., Ltd.

All rights reserved. No portion of this book may
be reproduced, stored in a retrieval system,
or transmitted in any form or by any means,
electronic, mechanical, photocopying, recording,
or otherwise, without written permission from the
publisher. For information regarding permission,
please contact info@reycraftbooks.com.

Educators and Librarians: Our books may be purchased
in bulk for promotional, educational, or business use.
Please contact sales@reycraftbooks.com.

This is a work of fiction. Names, characters, places, dialogue,
and incidents described either are the product of the author's
imagination or are used fictitiously. Any resemblance to actual persons,
living or dead, is entirely coincidental.

Sale of this book without a front cover or jacket may be unauthorized.
If this book is coverless, it may have been reported to the publisher as
"unsold or destroyed" and may have deprived the author and publisher
of payment.

Library of Congress Cataloging-in-Publication Data is available.

ISBN: 978-1-4788-6819-4

Printed in Guangzhou, China.
4401/0120/CA22000004

10 9 8 7 6 5 4 3 2 1

First Edition Hardcover published by Reycraft Books 2020

Reycraft Books and Newmark Learning, LLC, support diversity and the
First Amendment, and celebrate the right to read.

LET'S SWAP

FOR A DAY

Shu-Ti Liao

I am Alphie.

This is my best friend, Nini.

RO457385138

Sometimes we are jealous of
each other's life.

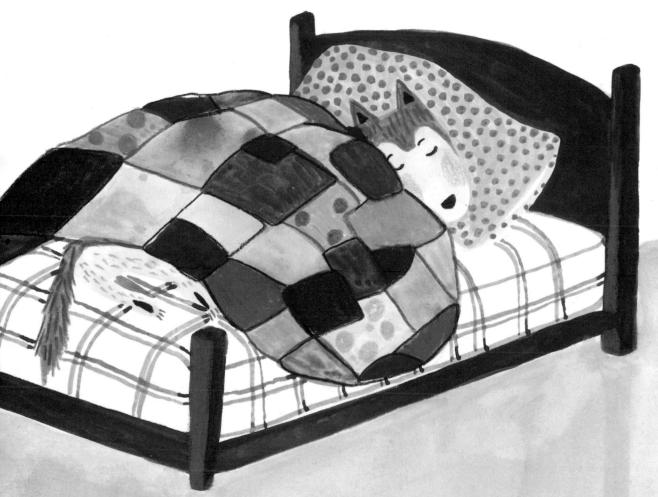

So we decided to swap for a day.

Guess what I did in the
morning on swap day?

Nothing but sleep until noon.

And Nini?
Nini danced all the way to school
with a big smile on her face.

Guess what I did in the
afternoon on swap day?

I swam in the sun,

played frisbee in the park,

and hid daddy's toupee.

And Nini?

She concentrated on
what the teacher said,

drew a portrait,

and played with her classmates.

EVERYTHING WAS WONDERFUL!

Until . . .

I was starving, but there were only bones
to eat and I didn't like the way they tasted.

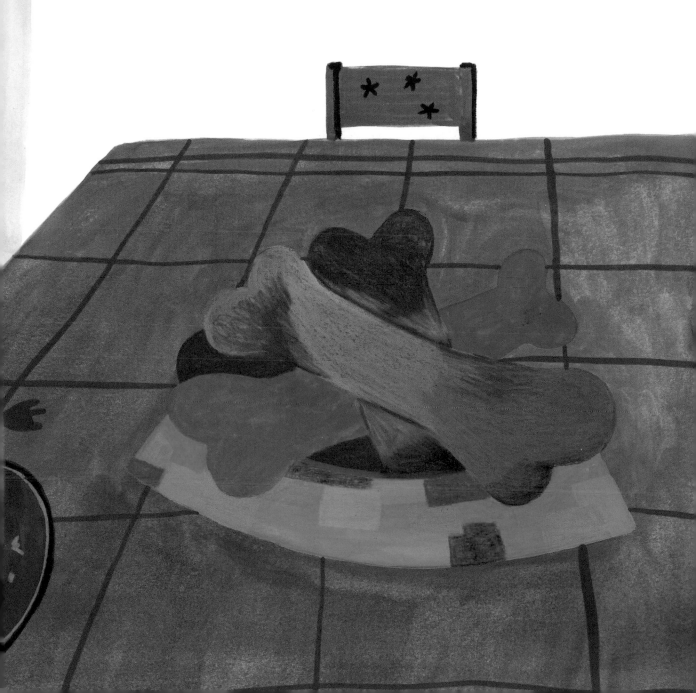

Nini was starving, too.
But she only had vegetables.
She didn't like them, either.

Things were getting worse . . .

"I don't want to poop outside!" I said.
Nini, on the other hand, really wanted
to do it in the grass—not in a bathroom.

So we both ran to the door.

Ahhh!

We're glad to be ourselves again!

SHU-TI LIAO

Shu-Ti Liao loves to draw and laugh. Her books are inspired by funny or interesting life experiences. She was awarded First Prize for England's Macmillan Prize for Illustration for her book *Adventure at Night*.